ALISTAIR HIGHET WITH ILLUSTRATIONS BY ETIENNE DELESSERT

LUCAS

CREATIVE
PAPER BACKS

Published by Creative Paperbacks, 123 South Broad Street, Mankato, Minnesota 56001; Creative Paperbacks is an imprint of The Creative Company. Designed by Rita Marshall

Library of Congress Cataloging-in-Publication Data

Highet, Alistair.   Lucas / by Alistair Highet ; illustrated by Etienne Delessert.
Summary: A young man and his dog become lost in the snowy forest, but just when it looks like they will not survive, Lucas, the dog, finds the way home.
ISBN 0-89812-014-4 (pbk.)
[1. Survival—Fiction. 2. Dogs—Fiction.] I. Delessert, Etienne, ill. II. Title.
PZ7.H543975 Lu 2000   [Fic]—dc21   98-050907

First Edition   9 8 7 6 5 4 3 2 1

LUCAS

I grew up in Nova Scotia, on a peninsula of rock that jutted out into the Atlantic Ocean. It was a wild place, with black spruce trees and granite boulders and a harsh, salty wind that roared in from the open sea to tug at my hair.

It has been many years since I last saw that place. Now I live in a different country, in a cottage where I write stories. When I do think of home, though, I think first of a cold February day, and how my dog, Lucas, saved my life.

ur town was remote, a half day's drive from Halifax. A handful of wooden houses on the rocks were connected by a road that wound around the coast, then swung up the hill toward the highway. There were no movie theaters or playgrounds, and no library.

Instead, as a young man, I passed the time walking the white sand beach with Lucas, picking up the strange shapes of wood that drifted in to shore. The beach was at the foot of the cliffs, near my house. In the autumn, the blueberry bushes that covered the cliff tops turned bright red, so as far as the eye could see, the coastline was red against the blue of the sea and sky.

There was a flat rock at the foot of the cliffs where the waves struck with a boom. On his stomach, Lucas

would crawl out to the edge of the rock to growl at the waves. It was his duty, he believed, to preserve me from the incomprehensible movement of the water. When a wave smacked the cliff, sending a pillar of foam above our heads, he pinned his ears back and barked at the sea.

Lucas could swim—I taught him—but he didn't like to, and it upset him when I plunged into the waves. I would turn, out there in the sea, and call for him to follow. But he stayed rooted to the sand, yelping after me.

Often, sea lions came into our cove to feed on the herring. They would drift slowly inland on the swell to stare at the barking dog and the pale man chopping through the water.

"Okay, okay," I would call back to Lucas when I couldn't stand the noise any longer. When I returned to shore, I would stride back and forth on the hard-packed sand to dry in the sun while Lucas followed close behind, his wet nose tapping the back of my knee.

It was a time in my life when I thought all day long about what was going to happen to me if I didn't leave the village.

●

ucas was my sister Fiona's dog, really. A mongrel, he looked like a small German shepherd, with wolf gray fur and small ears.

Fiona brought him home when he was a puppy, and he slept in front of her bedroom door, down the hall from the room I shared with my brother. But Lucas soon became the favorite of our family. He was, in fact, the only member of the family that we all felt comfortable talking to. We were a reserved people.

At night, my father, a Scottish man, would put on his flat cap and take Lucas for a walk. "Come on, son," he would say, in the Glasgow tone he reserved for his private thoughts, and they would walk out under the street-

lights. My father always called Lucas "son" when they were alone.

My mother spoke to Lucas in the long afternoons out there on the peninsula. She would gaze out the window at the open bay and talk about her home in Scotland, which she missed, and of what it would be like to move to a city like Toronto or Montreal.

I saw her take Lucas' face in her hands one afternoon. "You wouldn't like the city would you?"

●

When I was eighteen, I went away to England to attend university. London was a gray, dark city. In the afternoons I sat in stone lecture halls and listened to professors speak of Shelley and Keats, the death of language and the twilight of reason.

At night, I walked the wet, cold streets of London by myself. Once, at the pond at St. James, I stood on the bridge to watch the pink moon rise over the tower of Horse Guards. A family of white geese drifted toward me, quacking for bread. When they saw I had none, they turned away. The rude geese and the tiny pond made me long for the open sea outside my window at home.

So, only a few months after beginning university, I packed my clothes and sold my books. I bought a one-way ticket to Halifax, and five hours later, the plane touched down on the runway's hard-packed snow.

I hitched a ride as far as the village, then walked the empty road to my house. There was no one home except Lucas, who met me at the door. We sat in the living room, my bag at my feet, and waited for my parents.

●

That winter, Lucas and I roved the beach as we always had. At night, around the dinner table, it was quiet. "Now what?" my father asked me one night. "What are you going to do?"

"I don't know," I said, and that was as far as the discussion went.

●

I t was a cold winter, and a gray one. It rained every morning, and then the rain froze like glass on the snow. In the afternoon, the sun melted the ice, leaving a slick film of water on the streets and snowbanks.

One early February day, it snowed off and on. Lucas and I spent the morning inside the house, but by about two o'clock, I was restless and thought we should go for a walk.

Usually, we went to the beach, but that day I needed a change. For days, I had been thinking about Suzy Lake, a large pond that I knew of, deep in the woods to the north of our village. The lake was surrounded by pines and spruce trees. In the winter, the surface froze so thickly that a person could walk across it.

"To the lake?" I asked Lucas as I put on my boots and coat. He pawed anxiously at the door. When I opened it, he shot out toward the beach. But I called him back and led him up the road and into the trees.

I knew the path to the lake well. Once, it had been a logging trail, and it was clearly marked. The path followed the power lines for half-a-mile before it narrowed and angled north into the dense brush.

As we started along the trail, I could hear in the distance the faint sound of cars and trucks passing along the Trans-Canada Highway, about five miles ahead. The highway cut through the woods, and the wet, whooshing sound of the traffic was like a beacon. To get to Suzy Lake, we had to cross the highway.

For the first few minutes, as we trudged through

the snow, Lucas played a kind of game with me. He would dash ahead into a white stand of birch trees, then stand motionless, waiting. He seemed to think he was invisible, but his bright eyes gave him away.

"Come on, you silly dog," I called.

Snow began to fall again. Thick white flakes drifted down like butterflies, twirling in the air.

The logging trail narrowed and turned north. The freezing rain of the past weeks had made the trail slippery, and it was hard to get solid footing. So, keeping the trail in sight to guide us, we stepped into the deep snow to the right and pushed ahead, into the woods.

There were blue jays above us, their blue markings bright against the white branches. The heavy birds hopped from branch to branch, shaking loose rivulets of snow that fell on our heads.

The air was cold, and the sky was an ominous gray, but I was determined to make it to the lake. I rubbed my hands together briskly and stuffed them in my pockets, but they remained cold, despite my warm gloves.

After awhile, I stopped to catch my breath in a thicket, and the branches around us filled with chick-adees. The little birds came within inches of us. Un-afraid, they pipped at us conversationally.

"Hello," I said quietly.

We continued on and soon came across a deer path.

It was narrow but easy to walk on, so we took it. The logging trail was still visible, but it was farther away now —through the trees. The snow began to fall steadily, the flakes smaller, as we climbed into a part of the woods I didn't know.

Lucas heard a sound. His ears straightened and he paused. He glanced at me, then stared up the deer path.

"What?" I asked him.

He didn't move, just stared straight ahead, with his ears alert.

"Come on!" I commanded, continuing. He followed. A few more steps up the trail, I heard it too: a faint murmur in the distance. It sounded like an argument, a group of lost hunters perhaps, arguing over which direction to take.

As we carried on, though, it became clear that the sound was not human. Something was squabbling in a language I didn't understand.

We got closer. I was wary. There was a clearing just over the rise. Lucas looked up at me, his back legs quivering. I patted his head to reassure him, and we started up the snow-covered slope. We reached the crest and peered down into the clearing.

A congregation of black crows stood under the gray sky on an open blanket of fresh snow. Dozens of them, in a large circle, rocked back and forth, clacking their beaks. "Caw-caw-caw," they went. The noise was deafening.

In the center, two of the birds stood facing each other. They ruffled their collars and hopped, up and

down, in a twisted dance.

"Cruck-cruck-cruck," the circle chanted.

Above, in the bare treetops, more of the black birds flapped like rags. The crows had convened a parliament in the wilderness.

Suddenly, with a sharp growl, Lucas charged at them, speeding past my legs. "No," I shouted, and grabbed for him, afraid the wild crows would tear him to pieces, but Lucas sped into the circle. The birds wheeled away with a powerful rush of wings.

Now Lucas stood in the center of the empty circle. Above him, the treetops were dense with angry black birds. I expected them to fall on us like a pack of wild dogs at any moment.

"Come on, Lucas," I said, eyeing the trees of crows.

"Human, Human," the birds cursed us. "Dog-Dog."

We didn't look up as we walked beneath the birds. Only when they were far behind did I turn. With a sudden gust of wind, the crows rose in a mass of black. They circled over our heads, then raced across the pale sky and out of sight.

We sat on a big rock for a few moments. "Strange," I said to Lucas, and rubbed his back. Much of the afternoon had now passed. I could hear the rush of traffic on the highway, though, sounding very close.

We carried on. The trail soon curved through a large stand of spruce trees, and we rounded a corner. There, blocking the trail ahead of us, was an upturned white Ford Cortina.

The car was silent, the doors flung open, the win-

dows smashed. I approached it slowly, afraid of what I might find. The windshield was also shattered and the red upholstery was rotting with mold and was pitted where animals and weather had torn away at it.

But there was nothing inside, no trace of a driver. It had clearly been there for years.

"But who drove it here?" I asked Lucas. He glanced at me, then nosed inside the car's open door, sniffed, and backed away. We left the upturned car behind and kept on going.

The sky was now a dark, icy gray. The delicate snow of the early afternoon had turned to a wet sleet that rained steadily down. We had been walking for two hours and had less daylight left than that. When the sun fell below the trees, the temperature would plummet fast, and I was cold already. We had gone far enough.

"Let's go back," I said abruptly.

I turned to the left and headed toward the logging trail that would guide us home. But when I pushed through the spruce trees' black boughs, the trail was nowhere in sight. I pressed on, certain I would find it at any moment. But every time I pushed through the next group of trees, I found only a new expanse of snow.

"Where is it, Lucas?" I asked.

I looked around for a moment, thinking. One sure way to get home was to keep walking north to the highway. When we reached it, a passing car would stop and pick us up.

So we trudged north, toward the sound of the cars.

The woods had become quiet, except for the patter

of sleet on the branches above. No more chickadees flitted through the trees. I knew what that meant—snow, and a lot of it.

Lucas didn't seem to mind. His tongue hung out and his eyes were crusted with snow. He seemed to smile, and I took his face in my hands and told him he was a good dog.

Shortly, we came to a ridge. Below us was a ravine of spruce trees. I could hear the speeding cars, just beyond the trees on the other side of the valley. Once we got across, I was certain the highway would be in sight.

Down we went. At the bottom, the snow was knee deep. I started across, brushing the spruce boughs, heavy with snow, aside with my arms. Each step was difficult now and my heart pounded with the effort. Lucas fol-

lowed, leaping awkwardly from one of my deep footprints to the next.

I was about halfway across when a rush of cold
sent a sudden and numbing chill through my body. My
feet had crashed through ice beneath me. I gasped as both
boots flooded with frigid water. I took another step to
steady myself and crashed through the ice again. Icy
water raced up my legs.

I had stumbled into a partially frozen swamp. I
lunged for a small spruce tree but fell once more, sinking
to my waist. The water was so cold it hurt.

"No," I shouted, and for the first time in my life I heard fear in my voice. I reached for the tree again. This time I grabbed hold and pulled myself next to its trunk. There, I lay panting. Lucas licked my face.

"Not now!" I shouted.

How deep was the swamp? I didn't know. It didn't matter. I crawled back to the foot of the ravine, with Lucas close behind.

We would follow my footprints home, I thought, step by step.

Looking ahead, however, I saw that my footprints were just a blur. Newly fallen snow had filled them. I turned around. It would have to be the frozen swamp, even if it meant crossing it on my hands and knees.

"We can do it," I said to Lucas.

But barely had I spoken those words when a terrible truth became clear to me. From where I stood, I could hear the highway traffic passing to the south.

That couldn't be! The highway was north.

I turned to face what I believed was north, and again I heard the faint whoosh of cars in front of me. The sound was just as strong. In fact, it was the same.

I turned to the east—maybe it was north—and I heard the sound of cars.

I spun in a crazed circle until I was dizzy. Every way I turned, I heard cars. The whoosh of the highway was bouncing around among the trees and rocks, reverberating off the snow so that now the sound came from the north, now from the south.

The highway was a mirage. Any direction I chose,

the haunting sigh of its traffic would likely lead me deeper and deeper into the woods.

Nobody knew where we were. Nobody knew we had gone for a walk. Nobody would think to look for us. When they did start to look, they would comb the beach. Nobody would ever think to search for us here. Night would come, and we would not live to see morning. That much I knew.

"I'm lost."

The words fell from my mouth. At first, they almost seemed funny. Then the truth hit me.

I plunged into the forest, away from the swamp, as fast as I could run. "Help!" I screamed. I stumbled over a fallen tree and dragged myself up, racing into the darkness. Lucas chased through the snow after me.

On and on I ran, with Lucas at my heels, until I tripped and fell through a cold fence of spruce limbs and icy snow.

Lucas trotted up to where I lay and pawed at my frozen hair. He stuck his nose in my ear. That brought my head up. I took his collar in both hands and looked into his dark eyes.

"We're lost, old friend!" I cried, and draped my arms around his neck.

Perhaps he had known this before I did, because he immediately jumped back. With his ears high and his hind legs trembling, he looked squarely at me.

"Home," I said. "Take us home, Lucas."

He paused, then tucked his tail between his legs and sped off into the trees. I pulled myself up to follow. He

stopped a few yards away to make sure that I was coming and ran off again into the dark woods. He became little more than a shadow, which I chased as fast as I could.

Something about the world changed for me in those moments. I stopped thinking and just tried to keep pace with the animal in front of me. Now, Lucas was the master. He was in charge.

He didn't wait for me, but dashed through a maze of dark and whirling snow. Every now and then, he stopped to sniff at a tree. His sense of smell, that which I was blind to, was our only hope.

"Lucas," I called, disoriented and exhausted, "I have to stop." But he wouldn't let me. He barked sharply when he looked back and saw me leaning heavily on a bank of snow.

Lucas willed me on.

As if a dream, his gray shadow raced through the forest. I saw nothing but a blur of black spruce whipping past my face until a form loomed up in front of me. It was as large as a pale, granite rock. I raised my hands to stop myself, but I crashed into it with full force.

It was the upturned Ford Cortina.

"Lucas," I gasped.

He wouldn't rest, and I followed: past the broken circle of hard snow where the crows had warned us, and through a glistening cathedral of birches. I followed until I saw, glittering beneath my boots, the ice of the logging trail, and in the distance, through the treetops, the silver glint of streetlights.

Minutes later, I opened the back door of our house

and fell into the warmth of the hallway. Lucas followed

me inside, went straight to my sister's door, curled up and

fell asleep..

⬤

I never told anyone about that day.

The rest of the winter, when Lucas and I went to

the beach, we sat side-by-side on a driftwood log

and looked silently out to sea. When he was ready to

leave, he rose, shook the sand out of his coat and looked

squarely at me. He was never a dog in the traditional

sense after that. We were equal partners.

There were other changes in me—subtle ones. I

began to read again, and that summer I applied to a college in Montreal and was accepted. In the fall, I left home for good.

When I look back at that time of my life, I think of Lucas.

He's dead now; he died seven years ago. I was far away when I heard about it. He was with my mother on the back lawn, and she tells me that she held him in her arms.

●